★★★★★★★★★★★★★★★★★★★★★★★★

AMAZING ESME

and the Sweetshop Circus

Tamara Macfarlane

ILLUSTRATED BY

Michael Fowkes

h

Hodder
Children's
Books

A division of Hachette Children's Books

STAINED GLASS WINDOW
RECIPE

INGREDIENTS

(MAKES ONE CARAVAN WINDOW

OR

6 TREE DECORATIONS)

ASK AN ADULT TO HELP YOU BAKE THIS
DELICIOUS CIRCUS TREAT

- 175 g plain flour, plus extra for flouring the rolling pin

- zest 1 juicy orange

- 100 g butter, cold, cut into chunks

- 50 g golden caster sugar

- 1 tbsp milk

- 12 fruit-flavoured boiled sweets in as many colours as possible

- about 120cm thin ribbon, to decorate

INSTRUCTIONS

1. Turn the oven on – about gas mark 4 or 160 degrees C.

2. Throw the flour into the biggest bowl that you can find and grate the juicy orange zest on top.

3. Squeeze the butter chunks between your fingers (only if you've washed your hands!) until it's all squashed up and in bits, then grab handfuls of flour and squish it all together.

4. Splash in the milk and sprinkle in the sugar.

5. Squish it all together a bit more.

6. Spread flour all over the table, turn the bowl upside down and knead the mixture for a bit until it all sticks together.

7. Put it back in the bowl and put the bowl in the fridge.

8. When you are bored of waiting, take it back out and roll it as flat as a pancake. Cut it into strips.

9. Pretend the strips are window frames and lay them out beautifully in a sort of criss-cross pattern on some parchment paper.

10. Bash the sweets a bit inside their wrappers until they are crushed and sprinkle lots into the square spaces.

11. Bake for 15-20 minutes until golden brown with melted middles.

12. Don't touch — however much you want to eat them. They will be so hot at this stage that they'll burn a hole in your tongue!

13. When they have cooled use a mixture of icing sugar and water to stick them to the caravan – or ribbon to hang them from the tree.

Text copyright © 2012 Tamara Macfarlane
Illustrations copyright © 2012 Michael Fowkes

First published in Great Britain in 2012
by Hodder Children's Books
This paperback edition published in 2013

1

A Catalogue record for this book is available from the British Library

ISBN – 978 0 340 99994 3

Printed and bound in Great Britain by
Clays Ltd St Ives plc, Bungay, Suffolk

The paper and board used in this paperback by Hodder Children's Books
are natural recyclable products made from wood grown in
sustainable forests. The manufacturing processes conform to the
environmental regulations of the country of origin.

Hodder Children's Books
A division of Hachette Children's Books
338 Euston Road, London NW1 3BH
An Hachette UK company
www.hachette.co.uk

Contents

★ ★ ★

For my grandmothers, Queen Bee,

Grandmother Elspeth and Jocelyn Bell.

Three amazing women.

Introduction

★ ★ ★

'I love you, Donk,' Esme calls across the circus tent.

She is perched high up on the trapeze stand like a sequinned bird ready to fly. Far beneath her crowds of people bustle into their ringside seats.

The sides of the big top ballooned out as it breathed all the people in. With them came the tantalisingly sweet smells of toffee apples, candy floss and popcorn. Esme looks down from her hideout tucked high up in the darkness to see face after face peering up at the high wire.

Suddenly, with a crash
of cymbals . . .

A drum roll . . .

A flash of lights . . .

In strides the ringmistress . . .

Her whip cracks . . .

And in from the starlit
night, the circus appears!

Acrobats soar through the
curtains with jewelled flashes,
lightning quick, cartwheeling
like fireworks. Their bodies
are sparklers, drawing bright
pictures against the dark.

Clumsy clowns tumble in circles,
throwing custard pies
between stilt walkers' legs.

Fire jugglers' fingers
play with flaming streaks
of gold, lighting up the
plumed palomino horses as they cavort
through the curtains to glow in the warmth of
the audience's applause.

Above, Esme and Donk watch and wait. A
circus girl and her trusty pet mule moments

away from their first ever real-life circus performance. The performance that they have been practising for the whole of their lives.

Only seconds are left.

The ringmistress's whip cracks again, once, twice, three times. Band music swirls up and sends Esme twirling along the high wire. Donk steps carefully on at the other end. Hoof in front of hoof in front of careful hoof, he quick-steps towards Esme. Meeting in the middle, they dance together under the painted stars of the circus tent.

Cries of amazement ring out from below. Esme flips on to Donk's back and balances there on one leg as he prances, high-hoofing, along the high wire to the top of the trapeze stand.

Donk hooks his hooves over the waiting trapeze and leans forwards.

His sequinned unitard shimmers in the lights as he kicks out his hind legs.

His fat, furry body becomes sleek as he sweeps above the crowds and his extra-large ears stream out elegantly behind him.

The crowd are on their feet.

Donk flips over the trapeze and swings back to collect Esme.

She waits for the right second to leap, and sighs with silent relief as her hands feel Donk's furry legs. They somersault over the trapeze four times before swinging back up to the safety of the stand.

The audience beneath them clap until their hands hurt, stamp until their feet ache and cheer until their throats are dry.

Esme and Donk, hoof in hand, take to the high wire to bow. Their smiles are as wide as the circus tent.

ONE
★ ★ ★

Entertaining Esme

'BORED, BORED, BORED, BORED, BORED,' chanted Esme, hanging upside down from the high wire the next morning.

'Every day it's just PRACTICE, PRACTICE, PRACTICE!' Esme flung her arms down dramatically.

'It's just the same thing, DAY AFTER DAY!'

Esme shook the rehearsal timetable in her hand.

Day	Morning – 2 hours	Afternoon – 2 hours
Monday	Somersaults	Hanging upside down
Tuesday	Balancing on one leg while juggling eggs	Balancing on the other leg while juggling water bombs
Wednesday	Backflips	Cartwheels
Thursday	Trapeze and high wire	Animal kindness training/ costume design
Friday	Circus routines	Animal care

'It's only Monday and I'm sick of this already; I will certainly have died of boredom by Friday afternoon and then my mother will be sorry.'

Donk looked up from his cosy spot nestled in the soft sawdust of the circus ring and snorted loudly to warn her that her mother was coming.

'I don't care, Donk. I'm bored and it's her fault. She keeps making me practise but we don't need to any more. Did you hear the crowds cheering for us last night? They loved us. Besides, I'm a natural circus performer. So I'm going to tell my mother, no more rehearsals.' Esme swung backwards and forwards, becoming more indignant with each sentence.

Esme had been born in the circus ring. Her mother had given birth to her while swinging from a trapeze. Fortunately Esme had survived the fall as her father had dropped the reins of his horse and reached up to catch her. Thunderous applause at this amazing act had welcomed her into the world and Esme had been desperate to perform from that moment on.

'ESME, are you whining? Do I hear a child of mine whining?' Esme's mother pulled a wagon full of geese into the room behind her.

Esme was outraged. She'd heard other children whining – 'I want an ice cream now,' 'I'm not comfortable,' 'That pig smells' – and she couldn't bear it.

'But—' Esme started.

'But nothing,' her mother continued. 'How you have time to whine with so much around here to be done, I just don't know! Please go and tidy your caravan – it looks like a pigsty. And then go and clean the actual pigsty.'

'But—' Esme tried again.

'No buts, Esme. The circus pigs can't perform covered in mud. Then come and help me with these geese. They've been injured trying to escape a fox attack and the local farm has asked us to look after them. Your father is building a pen for them.'

'But—' Esme started once more.

'ESME!' screeched her mother. 'Get to work now or I will empty your caravan

into the duck pond and you will have to fish
for your things!'

Esme somersaulted
down from the high
wire and ran to save
her caravan.

After heaving
Donk over the half-
door by his ears, she
looked around at the
mess in front of her. She loved her gypsy-style
caravan. She loved the cosiness and clutter.
Jars of circus make-up lay with lids off on
a small table. Little pots of glitter sparkled
on the window ledges. Spare sequins
had scattered from her costumes and lay
twinkling on cushions, rugs and chairs.

Last night's pyjamas and tonight's tiger-print leotard embraced on the floor. Circus books were everywhere: open, closed, spine up, face down, on her bed, in her tiny kitchen, on the corner of her miniature sitting-up bath.

'Come on, Donk, I suppose we had better tidy up,' said Esme as she scooped up everything that she could fit in her arms and flung it all on to her bed. She threw her duvet over the pile and then firmly closed the polka-dot curtains that separated her bed from the rest of the caravan.

'Good, that's done then.' Esme flopped down on to her small raggedy sofa and wondered how to get out of cleaning pigsties, mending broken geese and, most of all, rehearsing. Donk curled up at her feet and snored.

'Oh, Donk, wake up and help. I'm bored, bored, bored!!!!!' Esme poked him gently with each word.

'Esmeeeeeeeee, that is *it*!' Her mother's voice leapt in through the caravan door, closely followed by the rest of her mother. Donk woke up and leapt to his feet.

'Only boring people get bored and I will not have a boring child. Find a way to make things interesting or I will do it for you. The clown's underpants need to be washed. The pigs are *still* dirty, the sawdust needs to be swept, the two hundred seats polished, the popcorn maker cleaned, the ice-cream machine washed out, the outdoor loos need scrubbing and that is just the beginning. I never ever want to hear the "B" word coming out of your mouth again! Nobody in the circus has time to be bored.' Esme's mother stormed out, trailing goose feathers behind her.

'Oh, Donk, why am I finding practising so b-o-r-i-n-g?' Esme whispered the last word as her mother frequently appeared out of nowhere at the worst possible moment. 'Maybe new costumes would help. Perhaps zebra print instead of tiger stripes? Or maybe some new tricks on the trapeze?'

Esme looked up at her favourite photograph hanging on the wall opposite. A black and white picture of Elenora, a world-famous Russian acrobat. Elenora was the other reason that Esme had wanted to become an acrobat. She had worshipped her from the moment that she had first seen her flying across the big top when she was four.

Clambering on to her table, Esme took down the photo and whispered a quiet plea to Elenora for help. Looking at the picture more carefully, she now noticed three animals waiting at the top of

the trapeze stand, partly hidden in the unlit darkness.

'Look, Donk, Elenora must have had animals in her acrobatic act too. You're not the only acrobatic animal in the world after all . . . although you are, of course, the best.' Esme kissed Donk on the top of his head and ruffled his ears. 'I'm sure that's a flamingo in the dark just behind her, next to a penguin and . . . a squirrel. Interesting, unusual choice . . . but that's it!' Esme scrambled on to her bed and rummaged through the pile of mess for a pen and a piece of paper. 'I've got it, Donk. We just need more animals for our act, then rehearsing won't be so boring! And I know just where to find them!'

TWO
★ ★ ★

Maclinkey Castle to the Rescue

Esme's letter was delivered to her cousins at Maclinkey Castle by the very same postal van that had delivered Esme there the previous summer. The postman sang to himself as he swerved round a family of lesser purple-crested frogs and stopped to let a herd of miniature Highland cows amble by as he made his way up the long castle driveway.

'Morning,' said the postman to Esme's cousin Magnus. 'Only one today and nothing

for your uncle. I'll keep a lookout for the snake-shaped box that he's been waiting for from Peru. Don't worry, I warned them not to open it by accident at the post office.'

'Thanks. Apparently it's the last pair of long-eared snakes on the planet. If Dad can't save the sick one they'll become extinct. Perhaps it'll arrive tomorrow.' Magnus turned the envelope over in his hand. 'It's from Esme,' he said.

Cosmo bounded up, snatched the letter and tore it open.

'She's my cousin; I should read it first,' said Cosmo.

'She's all of our cousin, actually, and as you were so horrible to her last summer it definitely shouldn't be you who gets to read it first!' said Magnus, taking the letter back.

Cosmo tried to snatch the letter back. 'I was not horrible to her. It was actually very kind of me to help her to do the fairground circus here so that her parents could see her perform with Donk. If they hadn't they would never have let her perform at Circus Miranda. This is probably a thank you letter from her to tell me how great I am for helping her.'

'That only happened because you tricked her,' said Magnus calmly.

'Can I see, can I see, can I see?' Gus, Esme's youngest cousin, jumped up and down trying to get the letter.

'What is all this nonsense about?' asked Mrs Larder, marching over to the squabble of boys.

Magnus handed the
housekeeper Esme's
letter, which she
began to read aloud.

Dear Magnus, Gus and Cosmo,
I am bored and I need some
more animals that would like to
visit and be in the circus
Please post them down.
They do not have to be tigers
I have enclosed some stamps and
a poster with our address for the
Summer.
Can't wait to see you!
Kiss the penguins and Mrs Larder's
whiskery chin for me
Love Esme
p.s Donk says 'Hi'
(I think)

'"Whiskery chin",' muttered Mrs Larder, stroking it. 'Really, that child.' She smiled fondly. 'When I think I used to change her father's nappies.'

'Never mind nappies,' said Cosmo. 'This means that we all get to go down and watch a real circus! We can't just send the animals on their own. Do you think Dad will let us go?'

'Let's go and make posters first,' Magnus answered. 'So we can see which animals want to join Esme's circus. Come on!'

THREE
★ ★ ★

Upside-down Animals

'I wonder if any of them will want to go,' queried Magnus as the boys jumped on to the helter-skelter slide and whizzed down to breakfast.

'Don't be silly. They loved being in the circus last summer and besides, it will be an exciting holiday for them,' Cosmo shouted as he leapt off the slide. He couldn't imagine any creature not wanting to see more of the world than the end of the castle drive.

Rhino after alligator after yak saw

the posters and grunted the message on.

Creatures twittered, squawked, gruffled and

mooed about the lights, the costumes and

the excitement of Esme's Fairground Circus

the previous summer. Very soon there was a

long queue of overexcited creatures winding

down the castle corridors.

Gus was just burying his face in a bowl of

porridge and trying to eat it from the inside

out when Mrs Larder bustled into the room

pulling fur and feathers out of her hair and

mouth.

'Why, might I ask, is almost every animal

on the Maclinkey estate now crammed into the

hallway? It's taken me half an hour just to get

over here from the laundry room! And why are

they all trying to balance one another on their heads? It can't be good for them. The webbed rhinoceros just tried to do a headstand and has got his horn stuck in the floorboards. His legs are swaying in mid-air and, quite frankly, it's a danger. What will your father say?'

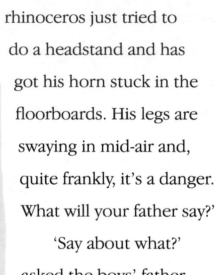

'Say about what?' asked the boys' father, Aubrey, sloping through the low doorway.

'Say about all the animals standing on their heads in the hallway,' Mrs Larder replied.

'I'm about to leave to visit my sick aunt in Glasgow and I could really do without all this extra fuss.'

Aubrey looked at her as though she had gone more than a little mad and turned to the boys.

'I need to go to London tomorrow, boys. As Mrs Larder is away, you will have to go and stay with Esme at the circus for a month while I do some research. White Siberian tigers have been going missing from a protected pack and I need to find out what is happening to them before they all disappear. We'll take the hot air balloon. Be on the turret roof before tea for take-off. Mrs Larder, could you bake us a chocolate cake for the journey, please?' he said, wandering out.

'Brilliant,' said Cosmo. 'Now we can take the animals down with us. We just need to get them on the roof early and hide them at the bottom of the balloon basket. Dad will be too busy thinking about Siberian tigers to notice.'

'But which animals?' said Magnus. 'They must all want to go if they've all lined up. How are we going to decide which ones to choose?'

'Let's have a talent contest and choose the most entertaining act. They'll have to perform to earn their place. Gus, go and tell them to start practising,' said Cosmo.

*

'Next!' yelled Cosmo as they sat on the judging panel. 'Please let it be good; I can't take much more of this. If I have to see one

more animal standing on one leg or trying to sniff its own bottom I'm leaving!'

Flapping through the door came Astrid the cormorant followed by three puffball penguins. Astrid was one of Cosmo's favourite creatures.

The boys watched as Astrid swooped down, opened her beak and swallowed a puffball penguin whole. There was a moment of silent shock from the boys before they launched themselves at the cormorant, desperate to retrieve the poor little puffball. Moments later, though, Astrid landed on the desk and spat the puffball out,

slimy but otherwise unharmed,
ending the act with a
beaky grin.

'FANTASTIC!'
yelled Cosmo.
'Dangerous and disgusting but
completely brilliant. Esme is going
to love it. Twenty million out of ten. This one
is going through.'

'You can't just put her through because she's your favourite animal. It wasn't that great. In fact, it was all a bit strange,' said Magnus, giving Astrid six out of ten.

Cosmo ignored him. 'Next.'

In trotted the kitchen pig; a unicorned pig called Mallow, spinning ten of Mrs Larder's best plates on his horn without dropping a single one. As his act finished, Mallow tilted his head slightly and the plates spun out and landed on the desk in front of the boys as though they were laid out on a table.

'That should
definitely be the
next animal that goes.
He can do all the washing
up for us as well.'

Mallow trotted round
to Magnus's side and
curled up gratefully by his

feet. Magnus scratched him in his favourite

spot just behind his right ear.

Cosmo looked at the cosy pair.

'Don't talk to me about favourites. We're

supposed to be taking good acts, not just our favourite pets!' said Cosmo. 'Next!'

'Wait, I don't think that we'll be able to fit any more animals in the basket. Anyway, we need to go and pack.'

'Can I carry the puffballs; can they be my act? Please, please, please. I won't even squash them.' And Gus slipped them into his pocket.

FOUR
★ ★ ★

A Trip to
the Circus

'Why haven't they written back?' Esme asked
Donk. 'It would've been two days since the
letter reached them and now we have to
go and perform the boring Flying Tigers
routine again. Even performing has become
boring!'

Esme chewed on a strawberry liquorice
straw and scuffed the ground with her
annoyed feet. Donk plodded loyally by her
side, hoping that she might throw a wine

gum his way. His ears felt heavier than usual as he listened to Esme moan.

'Where are the new animals for my act?' Esme called aloud. 'Someone, anyone, just find me some more animals. Pleeeaase.

'Argghhhhh,' she shrieked suddenly, as something landed in her bag of sweets. She peered in to see what it was, just as a puffball penguin popped up, busily munching on a bonbon.

'Arrrggggghhh,' she shrieked again.

Looking up for the cloud that was raining down penguins, Esme spotted a large stripy hot air balloon gliding down towards her.

It came down lower and lower and she began to recognise the three faces leaning over the side, waving.

'Look, Donk, they've come, they've actually come!'

Donk stuck his snout to the ground and plodded on. The balloon basket bounced several times as it hit the grass, before tipping out Magnus, Gus, Cosmo, a cormorant and a unicorned pig.

'ESME!' Magnus and Gus called, clambering over cases and running towards her for a hug.

'Oh, hi, Esme,' said Cosmo, crawling over a hamper to flick Donk affectionately on the ear. 'Wow, look at Donk. He's even uglier than he was last summer. I didn't think it was possible.'

Donk looked at Cosmo warily and then plodded as fast as he could towards Magnus, nuzzling into his side adoringly.

'We've brought some animals for your act,' said Magnus, putting Gus up on to his shoulders and scooping Mallow up under his arm.

'Mallow!' cried Esme delightedly, patting the unicorned pig that had fed her toasted marshmallows all last summer. 'Let's go and have tea. We'll go to Mum's caravan; there's more cake there. Come on, everyone, follow me.'

'But first I want to go and see that pirate circus ship on the river that we just flew over. It looks brilliant!' Cosmo said.

'You can't! They're trying to steal all our

Pirate Circus

Circus Miranda

customers. They only set up there because they saw all the people coming to our circus and now they stand outside our gates and tell everyone that their circus is much better. Mum is in a really bad mood at the moment because she's worried that people might believe them.' Esme led them into the largest of the caravans in the ring behind the big top.

'Hi, Mum,' she said. 'Look who's arrived for tea.'

FIVE
★ ★ ★

Tea and Cake

Esme's mother looked up from the small car she was mending for the clown's act and was slightly horrified by the sudden appearance of three boys, a unicorned pig, a cormorant and three small, strange-looking penguins squashing into her caravan.

'How lovely. Will you be staying long?' she asked politely.

'Well, we dropped Dad at the Natural History Museum in London to do some research. He sent us on to stay with you. I hope that's OK?' Magnus explained.

'He's researching lost white Siberian tigers. I think that he might be a while – the whole summer probably,' Cosmo continued.

Esme's mother's eyebrows rose a little higher. 'I see,' she said.

'But that's OK, isn't it, Mum? Uncle Mac did have me for the whole summer last year,' said Esme, squashing them around the table before her mother could change her mind.

Gus curled up on Esme's lap, Donk on Magnus's and Cosmo wrestled with Mallow while Esme's mother tried to fold Astrid on to the bench around the little table and started to hunt for a teapot.

'It's really not ideal. Your father and I

leave today to watch a new act that may be joining us. I hope that I can trust you to behave,' she said sternly.

The boys nodded eagerly.

'I suppose you'll have to join in Esme's circus lessons. That way you won't have time to get into too much trouble.' Spotting Esme's father, she beckoned him to the caravan.

'Henry, darling, would you please take the animals to their enclosure and then clear out one of the old caravans for the boys to sleep in? You can park it next to Esme's. I'll put the kettle on for when you get back.'

Esme's father winked at Esme and bear-hugged his nephews before wandering off obediently, carrying Mallow under one arm and juggling the three puffball penguins in the other hand. Astrid flapped alongside him as he whistled a circus tune to her. 'Cake, cake, cake!' yelped Gus, spying an enormous cream cake on the table.

'Say please,' said Magnus.

'And don't eat too much. You ate most of Mrs Larder's cake on the way here. I'm not looking after you if you're sick,' Cosmo warned.

'Please, please, please,' said Gus.

'Goodness, I just can't find the big teapot. I'm going to go and borrow one from Cook. Esme, please serve the cake. I won't be long.' Esme's mother hopped into the clown's miniature car and drove off.

Esme grabbed a pen and paper. 'Quick, while they're gone, let's work out how to put Mallow, Astrid and the puffballs into the new act.'

Esme nudged Donk with excitement.
'Donk, our new act is going to be
extraordinarily amazing. Even better than just
me and you, gorgeous as you are!' She patted
his snout.

Donk turned his large damp eyes and
downturned whiskers to her but Esme was
too excited to notice.

'I'm going to call the new animal act
Esme's Amazing Animal Allsorts. We'll need
new costumes. Just imagine the headlines,
the posters, the audience applause . . .'

Arriving back clutching an enormous teapot, Esme's horrified mother just caught the end of Esme's conversation.

'Absolutely not! What are you thinking, Esme? There is no way on this earth that any animals are going to join this circus without years of practice. Just wanting to be a circus animal isn't enough,' her mother continued.

'But . . .' tried Esme without much hope.

'No. That is my final word. Do not ask me again. I will not have animals endangered in my circus. Not ever. We have to go now.' Esme's mother poured tea into a flask. 'I am trusting you to behave. Lots of practice. See Cook if you need anything.' Her mother threw a feather boa into an old leather suitcase hugged Esme tightly. 'Love you,

darling,' she said, blowing the
boys a kiss and marching off to
collect Esme's father from
the top of the
circus tent.

'Oh dear,' said
Esme. 'That didn't
go very well. I
didn't want to tell
her yet. Never mind, we just need to teach
the new animals the routine really quickly. It
should be fine. We can use the practice tent
as soon as I finish my performance tonight;
we'll have an hour before supper. Then we
can try them out for a real performance while
Mum and Dad are away.' Esme poured tea
thoughtfully.

'But your mum just told you that the animals couldn't perform,' Cosmo said. Even he was slightly afraid of Esme's mother.

'I'm not going to get them to perform yet,' said Esme. 'My mother told me to go and practise and that is just what I'm going to do first thing tomorrow. Then later we can get them to perform so that when Mum and Dad get back they'll see how brilliant the act is. Remember last summer when they didn't realise how good Donk and I were until they saw us performing? She'll change her mind and they'll be really proud. I can't wait for you to see the circus and meet everyone . . . Oh no, I really can't wait.'

Esme had just noticed the time. 'Quick, we have to hurry! I have to go and get ready.

This evening's circus is about to start. Leave everything; we can collect it later,' Esme said, jogging towards the big top.

'But there's still cake . . .' said Cosmo, running back.

'Well, obviously bring the cake but leave everything else,' Esme called behind her. 'Quick, let's get you popcorn, candyfloss and ice cream from the stand.'

'Yes please, yes please, yes please!' shrieked Gus, who knew that there was no chance he was going to get any cake now that Cosmo was holding it.

'You'll have to go and find seats in the circus tent. You can't come behind the scenes until after you've seen the real circus for the first time. It spoils the surprise!'

SIX
★ ★ ★

Circus Stories by Firelight

Excitement lit up the boys' faces as they squeezed into the last three empty seats at the side of the ring.

All the stories that Esme had told them last summer came to life. They watched as each extraordinary act flew out far beyond their imaginations, then swung back up so close that the boys reached out to touch them.

With a drum roll, there was Esme, dancing high above them in her Flying

Tigers costume. A different Esme from the
one that had left them moments before. A
new, neat Esme, with tidy hair in a ponytail,
accompanied by an elegant Donk. A Donk
with dancing hooves and beautiful moves.

'Esme, Esme, Esme!' Gus called, waving
wildly.

She winked at them as she and Donk

took a final bow to rapturous applause and
disappeared.

Minutes later, Esme popped her face
through the curtain, 'Quick, follow me.'

Esme dragged them out of the big top.
Under the light of the moon, she wiped
off her circus make-up and shook her
unruly curls, as they headed for the animal
enclosure.

'It's my job to lay the table for all the
circus acts each night. We eat outside under
the stars, unless it's raining and then we put
up a kitchen tent. Let's ask Mallow to lay the
table tonight.'

'Magnus, you must meet Mungo, the
animal trainer.' Esme introduced them and
left them talking and stroking and soothing

the animals while she rounded up the others for supper.

Mallow performed his plate-spinning act and finished by laying out thirty plates along the large table by the big camp fire. Gus and Esme raced around with knives, forks and spoons while Cosmo lay down on his back and stared up at the scattering of early evening stars.

When the rest of the circus acts had finished performing, the crowds buzzed out and swarmed towards the exits in a wave of excited chatter. From the back of the big top, unseen by the crowds, all the weird and wonderful circus acts wandered out. They arrived for supper as usual in various states of undress, half human again, half magical visions, scattering false eyelashes and laughter across the table.

Esme stood on Donk's back so that all the acts could see her.

'Hi, everyone. These are my cousins. They have come to stay for a while. Magnus, Cosmo and Gus, these are all the circus performers. This is Orlanda the acrobat and these are Grigorio and Ivan, the horse jugglers, and this is Velk, the strong man and this is George the clown. And . . .' Esme carried on round the table as great bowls of potatoes swimming in melted butter arrived followed by freshly roasted chickens nested in beds of sausages and jugs of delicious-smelling gravy.

Magnus, Gus and Cosmo melted into the

colourful crowd and talked and ate late into the night, warmed by the huge camp fire. They toasted marshmallows on the flames of the candles that lit up the table and gobbled up stories of circus life, of near escapes and even more amazing acts in far-flung circuses across the world, sure that their ears would never hear such a feast of tales again.

SEVEN
★ ★ ★

The Animal
Allsorts

Before they'd even had time to realise that
they'd been asleep, Esme woke them up
again.

'Morning. Time to
get up. We have to go
and practise the new act
now before breakfast.
We can't be late for our
circus classes or we'll be
in trouble.'

Magnus and Cosmo both pulled their duvets back over their heads.

'Fine. I'll practise without you this morning, but you'd better be ready for costume design at seven thirty. We have to design the new Animal Allsorts costumes. No one gets lie-ins in the circus. I'll come back and fetch you.'

Gus took Esme's hand. 'I'll help you, Es.'

Esme helped him to pull a jumper on over his pyjamas and they wandered out to the practice tent. The sawdust in the ring stuck to their dew-drenched feet as they led the animals gently up the ladder and on to the high wire.

'Well done, Mallow. For a strange-looking round pig you have very dainty trotters! No

need for any more practice today. That was
brilliant. I'm sure that if Mum had actually
seen you all she'd be really happy for you to
perform. We'll try it out tonight as a surprise
for everyone. Mum probably just said no
because she was still cross about me being
bored and hasn't realised how good you all

are. Let's go and get the boys and make our new costumes.'

Sitting round a table in Daisy Davina's caravan, sketching designs and stitching on sequins was not Cosmo's idea of fun but Daisy took no nonsense.

'Not good enough, darling! Those stitches will fall out in a second and we'll have a naked mule on the tightrope! Do it again. Carefully now.' Daisy handed the unitard back to Cosmo.

With each stitch, Esme grew more and more excited about trying out the new act while Donk grew more and more nervous. He watched quietly from a corner of the sofa as the final stitches were sewn into the new costumes. He sighed as Esme fussed over

Mallow in his candy-striped waistcoat. His eyelids drooped as she tied a bow tie round the pig's tail and stood back to admire him. Tears crept out from under his lashes as Esme dressed Astrid in a sparkling top hat and put false eyelashes on the puffballs. He heaved himself up and plodded away to hide his tears and worry.

He longed for it just to be the two
of them together again. He missed their
rehearsals, each new trick that they'd
mastered along the way and all the times
they'd stopped each other from falling. It
wasn't a performance or an act when they
were together, it was real – they were a team
– Esme and Donk, Donk and Esme.

'Stunning, darling. Simply stunning!'
cried Daisy. 'Turn a little to the left . . . and
a little to the right . . . then we do this with
your hair . . . too perfect, too perfect. So
charming!! Enchanting! The pink with the
blue and the shimmering . . . it is all just too

wonderful. Now, off you all go; I must tidy. Shoo, shoo.' Daisy flapped them out of her overflowing caravan. 'Go and find Donk. Amaze him with the new unitard!'

When Esme finally found him, he was curled up under the duvet, his hooves holding his ears down to cover his damp eyes. She took the duvet off his head and rolled him out on to the floor. 'Come on, you lovely heifer, we have to go and get ready. No time for sleeping now. Tonight is going to be the best performance Circus Miranda has ever had. When Mum hears about it she'll have to admit that she was wrong.'

EIGHT
★ ★ ★

Cormorants and Catastrophes

They took up their usual positions at the top of the trapeze stands and Esme called across to Donk as she did every evening.

Circus Miranda had sold out that night so the boys sat on buckets backstage and peered through the curtains at the audience waiting for Esme's Animal Allsorts to perform. They were entranced by Russian cossacks, laughed hysterically at George the clown and were delighted by the jelly jugglers before taking a deep breath ready for the daring trapeze and high-wire act.

On came the spotlights and up swept the music as Esme skipped out on to the high wire, cartwheeling on to Mallow's back and then twirling off to collect Donk. Mallow  and Donk faced snout to muzzle in the middle of the high wire as Esme back-flipped over them both, collecting Mallow on the way and placing him on Donk's back.

The crowd were on their feet shouting, 'More, more, more!' Astrid swept low over the audience then spun up to collect the first

penguin. She spat it perfectly on to Donk's waiting hoof just as Esme leapt on to Mallow and stood balanced on one leg. The second penguin landed safely and the crowd cheered on. Astrid swept in with the third penguin in her beak. The end was so close; the crowd so enthralled. The happiness in Esme's face lit up the whole tent as she imagined how proud her parents would be.

Swooping down towards Donk's waiting hoof, the last puffball reached out its little wing, missed and slipped past Donk.

Donk reached out desperately to try to catch it, causing the carefully balanced pyramid above him to wobble. Mallow hadn't had enough practice to know how to get his balance back, and slipped off Donk's back.

Donk caught the falling pig but the extra weight unbalanced him and despite years of practice, he slipped off the high wire.

Panic-stricken, Esme darted along to her waiting trapeze and, leaping on it, she dived down towards Donk. Her heart thundered as she reached out her arms until they ached. Her fingertips felt the rough hair of Donk's tail slip through them and her heart plummeted as she watched his yelping body fall down and down and down, way below into the sawdust.

He did not move as the crowd erupted around him.

People ran for the exits.

'Shocking!' yelled one.

'Dangerous!' yelled another, tipping penguins out of her skirt.

'Outrageous animal cruelty!' yelled others as they made for the emergency exit.

'I am going to tell the newspapers,' a man in a hat shouted, running out. 'This circus is extremely dangerous and everyone should know.'

NINE

★ ★ ★

Popcorn and Punishment

News of the accident travelled fast.

With faces full of thunder and fury, Esme's parents returned early the next morning and called an emergency circus meeting.

Magnus gently shook Esme awake. She lifted her tear-streaked face from Donk's fur, tucked the covers back around his bandaged body, kissed the tips of his ears as they lay still on the pillow and walked down the steps of the emergency hospital caravan they had set

Daily News

Circus act takes a
TUMBLE!!

full story and Pictures Pages 2 and 3

Shock as circus stunt goes wrong... read more

up the night before.

Magnus put a reassuring arm round her
as they walked to the gathering, barefoot in
the dewy morning grass, still dressed in their
pyjamas.

'Don't worry, Es, we all make mistakes,'
whispered Grigorio as the other acts looked
at her with sympathy.

Her mother was not feeling quite so kind.

She addressed the whole circus. 'I can only apologise to everyone here for my daughter's behaviour. This is the last thing that we need. The Pirate Circus on the river is already taking away our customers with their loud cannons and poor, badly treated animals. We are going to have a difficult time trying to get people to come back to Circus Miranda now that we have treated our animals with even less kindness. This morning a letter came from the animal inspector threatening to close us down. He arrives in two weeks for an inspection!'

Her mother turned to Esme and unrolled a large poster.

'You may well have ended one hundred and fifty years of Miranda family circus history

with your impatience. Your father and I have decided that we were silly to think that you could be trusted. You will not be allowed to perform any more. You are to do the lowest job in the circus instead. Esme, you must run the popcorn stand.'

Her mother thrust a horrible, ugly clown costume at her for her new role and stormed off. She was closely followed by Esme's dad, who shrugged his shoulders kindly and gave Esme a comforting look that said 'it's OK, I understand, but what can I do?' before picking up the suitcases to follow her mother

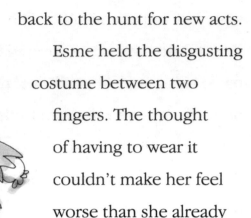 back to the hunt for new acts. Esme held the disgusting costume between two fingers. The thought of having to wear it couldn't make her feel worse than she already did about the injured animals but especially about Donk. Donk, who had been at her side for as long as she could remember. Donk, who had carried her to bed when she was too tired to walk and licked her face clean when she was too tired to wash. He had always been her safety net and now she had let him fall.

Tears trailed down Esme's face as she remembered the sight of Donk's body the night before, tumbling through the air as she tried to catch him. She covered her face with her hands as she remembered the day that he had been given to her with birthday balloons tied to his tail, his arrival at Maclinkey Castle last summer and all the wonderful, happy moments in between.

'What are you crying for?' Cosmo asked. 'Now you don't have to perform, you won't have to practise again. It was a great plan. Well done, Es. You got just what you wanted.'

'I didn't want this to happen. I would never want to hurt Donk or any other animal!

Now my mother is furious with me and Circus Miranda may have to shut down. I have to find a way to make things better for everyone.'

Esme tried hard to hold in her tears as she climbed back into the hospital caravan and stood next to Donk. He still hadn't twitched an ear or moved a whisker. She wiped her eyes on his pillowcase and whispered, 'Please get better. I am so, so sorry that I hurt you. I promise that I'll find a way for us to perform again, just as soon as you're ready.'

'Oh, stop being so wet, Esme,' said Cosmo. 'It's just you, you, you. We're here for the whole summer and it's really selfish of you to think that we're going to want to spend it sitting around here with a load of miserable, injured animals listening to you crying like a baby. I guess we're going to have to help you with this stupid popcorn stall now, so I'm going to look at the old caravans at the back of the circus ground to see if we can find a stall that we can actually make something of. I'm not spending my whole summer on that crusty old popcorn stand. I'll meet you there in five minutes if you can stop feeling sorry for yourself for that long.'

'Go on, Esme. Staying here won't help Donk get better any more quickly,' Magnus said as he peeled his cousin away from Donk and led her outside.

TEN
★ ★ ★

The Sweetshop Caravan

'I've found it,' called Esme. 'This is the one. There isn't too much mould and the kitchen part is still working. It just needs paint and some curtains. If we do it all up beautifully then my parents might be proud of me again and then when Donk gets better maybe one day we might be allowed back in the circus.'

'I don't think your mother is going to get over this in a hurry,' Cosmo said as he looked over the shabby old caravan. 'She looked like she'd swallowed a porcupine, last time I saw her.'

'She isn't really as tough as she looks. She just really cares about the circus, and all the acts are part of the big Circus Miranda family. She's just looking after everyone,' Esme said. 'I think that if we can save the circus she might forgive me.' Esme cartwheeled off the caravan roof and stood next to Cosmo.

That night's performance had been cancelled as no tickets had been sold. From where she was standing on the hill, Esme could see the long queue at the Pirate Circus ticket office by the river below. Inside her, all hope had dropped to her toes, but still she lifted up her chin.

'Let's drag the caravan to the circus gates. That way, the crowds going to the Pirate Circus will see us too. Once they smell the amazing sweets we are going to make, they might come back and try them. This could be the way to save the circus.' Esme began to push the caravan.

'One taste and they'll be hooked and if they aren't then we get to eat them all

ourselves, which is actually better,' added Cosmo.

'OK, we need a plan.' Esme hunted through her pockets and pulled out an empty paper bag and a pencil.

'You and your plans! Can't we just get on with it?' Cosmo asked, climbing in and out of the windows. 'We need windows . . .'

'We need lots of things,' said Esme. 'That is why we need a plan. We have to do this properly. Where on earth are we going to get glass for the windows?'

'I know what we can do for the windows, Es,' Cosmo said excitedly. 'We used to make these stained-glass window decorations with Mrs Larder at Christmas. We made frames from pastry and melted different-coloured fruit sweets in the oven. The sweets went all flat and you could see through them. The caravan windows are fairly small. I'm sure it would work.'

'Good idea, but we need paint first. Look how shabby this caravan is. I don't think that anyone has used it for at least a hundred years. We have to make it look like a sweetshop. Nobody will want to eat food out of it now. They'd probably get splinters in their tongues.'

Without a performance to watch or be in, a long empty evening spread out in front of them, providing the perfect opportunity to paint and clean. On the way to get paint, hammers and nails from the circus workshop, Esme and Cosmo checked on Magnus and

Gus, who were busy looking after the injured animals in the hospital caravan.  Magnus was full of excitement as Donk had finally opened his eyes and snuffled about until Gus had fed him some leftover popcorn. Esme kissed him on the snout delightedly.

'Magnus, do you think all the animals will be OK?' Esme stroked Donk's tangled mane.

'It will probably take some time but I'm sure Donk'll be fine. Mallow's leg is mending well and he should be up and about in a few more days. But please can you take Astrid out? She needs exercise.' Magnus gently held Donk's nostrils closed until he opened his

mouth for breath and Gus could pour some
medicine in.

Esme jumped around for joy at seeing
Donk move, and swung Gus up in the air. 'My
Donk moved, he moved. He's going to be OK!'

'Esme, please get out,' said Magnus.
'This caravan is too small for all this
overexcitement.'

Finally, reassured that Donk was on the mend, Esme kissed his snout one last time and tore herself away.

Desperate to be able to start making sweets and popcorn, candyfloss and ice cream, Esme, Cosmo, Gus and Astrid painted, polished, washed, scrubbed, hammered and swept the dirty old caravan into a mouth-watering sweetshop. Sunshine cast rainbows through the baked boiled-sweet windows.

Finally, as the large sign announcing 'Circus Treats and Circus Sweets' was finished, they put down their tools and looked at it proudly.

ELEVEN
★ ★ ★

A Recipe for Chaos

'Now we just need to learn to cook,' declared Cosmo. 'Let's get started! I get to make the first thing because it was all my idea and I'm starving after all that hard work.'

'We need recipes,' said Esme. 'Let's try this.' She pulled down a huge cookery book from the shelf. *Circus Treats and Circus Sweets* by Lucinda Larder. This will do.'

CONTENTS

STAINED GLASS WINDOW RECIPE

Ask an adult to help you bake this delicious circus treat.

Ingredients to collect:

makes one caravan window (or 6 tree decorations)

175g plain flour, plus extra for flouring the
     rolling pin
zest of 1 juicy orange
100g butter, cold, cut into chunks
50g golden caster sugar
1 tbsp milk
12 fruit-flavoured boiled sweets in as many
     colours as possible
about 120cm thin ribbon, to decorate

Instructions:

1. Ask an adult to turn the oven on. About gas mark 4
    or 160 degrees.
2. Throw the flour into the biggest bowl you can find and
    grate the juicy orange zest on top.
3. Squeeze the butter chunks between your fingers (only if
    you've washed your hands) until it's all squashed up
    and in bits, then grab handfuls of flour and squish it
    all together.
4. Splash in the milk and sprinkle in the sugar.
5. Squish it all together a bit more.
6. Spread flour all over the table, turn the bowl upside
    down and knead the mixture for a bit until it all
    sticks together.
7. Put it back in the bowl and put the bowl in the fridge.
8. When you are bored of waiting, take it back out and
    roll it as flat as a pancake. Cut it into strips.
9. Pretend the strips are window frames and lay them out
    beautifully in a sort of criss-cross pattern on some
    parchment paper.
10. Bash the sweets a bit inside their wrappers until they are
    crushed and sprinkle lots into the square spaces.
11. Bake for 15-20 minutes until golden brown with melted
    middles. Ask an adult to help you take your hot window
    frames out of the oven.
12. Don't touch, however much you want to eat them. They
    will be so hot at this stage that they'll burn a hole
    in your tongue!
13. When they have cooled, use a mixture of icing sugar and
    water to stick them to the caravan (or ribbon to hang
    them from the tree).

'Look, there's the boiled sweet window recipe!' Cosmo said, glancing over the instructions. 'We don't need these recipes,' he continued. 'We made perfect windows without any instructions. Recipes will just slow us down.'

He tossed the book aside, and grabbed the flour. He tipped it into the bowl, followed by seven eggs, a large bar of chocolate, a bag of sugar, and some jam.

'Cosmo, stop putting just any old thing into the bowl. We're supposed to be following a recipe and we haven't even decided what we're making yet!' Esme said, pulling more ingredients out of the kitchen cupboards.

'Oh, ignore the recipe. Let's invent a new pudding – we'll put in everything that we

love to eat and see what comes out.' Cosmo
opened a large bag of marshmallows and
poured them into the bowl. He unscrewed
the lid of a jar of honey and scooped it in
with his bare hands. He measured out a jug
of maple syrup and watched as the beautiful
auburn syrup slipped into the mixture. One
by one, he aimed strawberry after strawberry
at the bowl before taking down a bag of
unpopped popcorn kernels, a handful of
chocolate drops, four packets of different-
coloured jelly . . .

'Cosmo!' Esme said severely.

'Oh, you're so boring, Esme. You have no imagination. This could be the greatest pudding ever. It could be in the recipe book for the best pudding recipes that ever existed on earth and you don't even want to try it out . . . not even once . . .' Cosmo threw in a tub of cocoa powder and shook up a bottle of ginger beer until it overflowed into the bowl.

'I don't care about famous puddings, Cos. I just care about trying to save the circus. If I get into any more trouble my parents will probably sell Donk or something. Stop throwing things in. We have to do this properly. I have to be responsible!'

'Come on, Es, just one try. If it isn't the best thing that you have ever tasted then we'll do it your way. I promise. Even if it is the boring way and it won't be any fun.' Cosmo emptied in a little bottle of vanilla essence, some butter and a tub of cake decorations.

'OK, one try and that's it. If this doesn't taste good then you have to promise on Astrid's life that we do it my way.' Esme picked up a large wooden spoon and stirred the gooey mess. 'Actually, that's pretty good.

As long as you avoid the raw jelly and the popcorn kernels . . . It needs something though, something less sweet, something like . . . cornflakes. Then it will taste like chocolate crispy cakes and I love those.' Esme poured in the remains of a packet of cornflakes. 'And loads of cream. Everything tastes better with cream on top.' Esme poured in a tub of extra-thick double cream.

'Do you think we ought to write a list of the ingredients in case it really is amazing? If we don't we might never be able to make it again.' Esme stirred the thick mixture.

'Nah! We'll remember. Good cooks don't need recipes.' Cosmo reached in for a final lick, pulled out a large glob and flicked it straight at Esme.

'Arrrrrgggggggggggggggggh,' Esme shrieked and threw an egg at his head. He grabbed a half-empty bag of icing sugar and hurled it through the air at her. Sugar burst out all over them. Cosmo scrabbled around wiping sugar out of his eyes and grabbed Esme's ankles toppling her over, face first, into the large mixing bowl of goo.

Esme pulled her gungey face out of the bowl and charged at Cosmo, wrestling him to the floor. As soon as he landed she sat on his back, reached out for the bowl, and poured it

all down the back of his trousers.

She was up and out of the kitchen before
he could grab her.

Cosmo stood up slowly, squelching with
every move. Mixture trickled out from the
bottom of his trousers leaving a trail behind
him as he sloshed out to catch her.

'No more!' Esme yelped as he got closer.

'We'd better tidy up first. If anyone sees that mess we'll be in big trouble.'

They glanced back through the caravan at the empty packets, spilt honey, trails of popcorn kernels and squashed

marshmallows. There wasn't one tiny spot in the kitchen not covered in something very sticky.

'I'm not tidying up. I want to try out the ice-cream machine,' Cosmo replied. 'I know . . . GUS!!' Cosmo called over to the hospital caravan where Gus had been helping Magnus.

'Yup?' Gus stuck his head out of the door.

'I'll give you half a bag of toffees and a taste of the best ice cream ever made in the whole of the world just for doing a little teeny, weeny bit of tidying up.' Cosmo held out the bag of toffees.

'OK, I'll do it!' Gus ran more quickly towards them.

'Brilliant. Thanks, Gus. You're the best. We'll be back soon.' Cosmo threw a dishcloth towards him and walked away as quickly as he could with a bowl of cake mixture down his trousers.

'Hey, that's not fair. Gus didn't even make the mess.' Esme pulled on Cosmo's gooey sleeve.

'Fine, you stay here and help. I'm going to see if the ice-cream machine still works. If I have to follow a stupid recipe then it had better be for the best sundae ever!'

TWELVE
★ ★ ★

Sensational Sundaes

The ice-cream machine did work. Cosmo and Esme moved it to the Circus Sweets caravan in between baking cakes and designing new sweets; they created amazing ice cream sundaes, each one more extraordinary than the last.

'My new caramel-ripple, strawberry-scented, triple-layered lavender-biscuit and honeycomb ice-cream sundae is much better than anything that you could make, Esme.'

Cosmo ate large spoonfuls of it in front of Esme's face.

'Just you wait, Cosmo. As soon as we get all the customers back here, we're going to have a competition for the best ice-cream sundae and I bet you one day of doing all your jobs that I'll win.'

'I bet you two days of doing all your jobs that *I* win,' said Cosmo. 'Deal?'

'Fine then, two days. All jobs for the winning sundae.' Esme looked up. 'But it's my turn on the ice-cream machine.'

Cooking for the sweetshop swallowed up the whole of the rest of the week and helped to keep Esme's thoughts busy. They emptied the kitchen tent of supplies, picked apples from the trees, strawberries from the fields and blackberries from the bushes.

Within days, the scents of vanilla and chocolate drifted out across the circus grounds. The performers woke each morning to a wonderful new smell: mint and toffee, strawberry syrup and honeycomb, freshly baked cakes and cooling caramel biscuits.

While Magnus studied rare animal breeds and nursed the injured creatures in the hospital caravan, Esme, Cosmo and Gus studied recipe books and shelves of ingredients. They stirred and beat and mixed and cooked until each new sweet began to look more and more like the pictures in the recipe books. They filled jars with home-made strawberry bonbons, rainbow pips and lemon sherbets. They coated honeycomb in

velvety chocolate and poured caramel over anything that they could find.

Early each evening, Esme gathered up a little pocketful of goodies and hand-fed them to Donk as she told him stories of all the things that they would do together when he was better. She stayed by his side until he drifted off to sleep.

People all along the riverbank were drawn by the delicious smells across the grass to the small caravan. Their eyes feasted upon the rainbow display, jar after jar, each and every one full to the brim with the taste of happiness.

'Five lemon sherbet sticks, please.'

'Four candyflosses, two liquorice twirls and a caramel cupcake, please.'

'Two ice-cream floats, three honeycomb dreams, one jelly elephant, a strawberries-and-cream lolly and four monkey paw muffins, please.'

It was working. People were coming back to Circus Miranda. The children could hardly keep up with the demand.

Mallow was much better and he sat outside the caravan while Cosmo spiked cupcake after cupcake on to his horn, spinning each one as he iced them.

He soon became an expert in icing cakes in wild and wonderful ways.

His decorations became more elaborate; delicate sugar-spun circus girls balanced on iced prancing ponies, gold icing on a silver background. Red and yellow candy clowns

tumbled against pools of blue icing.

Esme stopped serving for a minute and
let her eyes wander over each heavenly tray.
A caravan full of delights that she had hardly
had time to try. She wondered where she
should start . . .

'Gus! What are you doing?' Esme asked in
horror as her eyes fell upon her cousin taking

great big licks on a large purple lolly and then thrusting it in front of a very mangy-looking tiger who was also giving it enormous licks.

'I'm sharing my lolly with a tiger. Why?' Gus looked confused. 'Cosmo told me to keep him here and feed him.'

Esme stepped outside the shop, turning the sign on the door to CLOSED. 'COSMO!' she yelled.

'What?' Cosmo stuck his head out of the tree that he was sitting in.

'Why is there a tiger in the sweetshop sharing a lolly with Gus?' Esme demanded.

'Oh, yeah, I forgot to tell you about that. He must have escaped from the Pirate Circus and come to find food.' Cosmo jumped out of the tree. 'He's really hungry so I thought I'd put him in the sweetshop and let him eat for a bit.'

Esme led Cosmo back inside the shop to find Gus. 'Look, he's been really badly treated . . . His fur is all straggly and mangy where he's been trying to get out of that tiny cage and he's a really strange colour too.' Cosmo lifted up clumps of fur to show Esme.

'We need to take him to Magnus. Some

of those scratches look really sore. Poor tiger,'
Esme said, stroking him. 'Gus, hold the lolly
out in front of you and walk down the steps
towards Magnus.' Esme went behind to herd
the tiger.

THIRTEEN
★ ★ ★

Tigers and Troubles

'This is definitely one of the rare breed of white Siberian tigers that Dad has been researching. We need to let him know that we've found him,' Magnus said, closing the animal encyclopaedia gently, using Donk's tail as a bookmark. 'But first of all we need to treat his wounds and find him some proper food to eat.'

Magnus set about cleaning the tiger's wounds. His face looked really cross for the

THE WHITE SIBERIAN TIGER

THE SIBERIAN TIGER'S fur lightens in the winter to help it to camouflage with the snow. It has the thinnest stripes of all the tiger sub-species. The stripes are chocolate brown. White Siberian tigers have blue or green eyes, unlike the regular Siberian tigers, which have yellow eyes. They can see six times better than humans at night and can run up to 50 miles per hour over the snow.

They are found mainly in the forests of Russia and China where they hunt for deer and wild pigs. Due to hunting and the destruction of their forest homes by humans, at one point there were only 50 Siberian tigers left in the world but now that they are protected their numbers have increased. However, they are still an endangered species.

first time ever, Esme thought.

'Just as I suspected,' a voice thundered up the caravan steps. 'Mistreated animals!' the voice continued.

Esme recognised the long face and clipboard of the circus inspector and leapt up to explain.

'This isn't our tiger. It has escaped from the Pirate Circus on the river. It ran away because they were being cruel to it. Look at the poor thing.'

'Oh, yes, and I suppose that strange donkey thing over there escaped from the Pirate Circus too, did it?' The inspector made furious notes on his clipboard. 'I've heard it all before. You can't fool me. I've just inspected that Pirate Circus and they didn't have any animals there. So that's the end of that excuse,' the inspector finished. 'I'll just sign this form and that will be the end of Circus Miranda and all the animal cruelty.'

The inspector looked up as Esme unrolled the large Pirate Circus poster that her mother had shown her when she'd been in trouble.

'Look, this is the tiger from their poster. The poster shows that they have animals. If you didn't see any it's because

they hid them away so that you wouldn't see how badly treated they are,' Esme explained desperately.

'Well … I don't know how that's possible. I always do very thorough inspections. However, that tiger does look very like the one on the poster. It's very strange. What tricks are you are up to, I wonder?'

Esme thought quickly. 'Are you hungry, Inspector? Why don't we make you something to eat before we show you the other animals? Unless you would prefer to see them first?' Esme prayed to Elenora for circus luck as she led the inspector over to Circus Sweets and sat him down at a little table outside. She hoped that if they fed him some of their sweet treats, they might soften his mood and stop him from closing the circus down.

'Well, since you asked, something sweet to eat would give me energy for the rest of the inspection.' The inspector's face lifted slightly at the thought. 'Though I have to say, it's not looking good for Circus Miranda so far.'

Cosmo had heard the news about the inspector and jogged over to join Esme.

'What's your favourite sweet, Inspector?' asked Cosmo, winking at her.

'Hmmm, I like toffees and wine gums and liquorice allsorts and chocolate éclairs and . . .' The inspector paused to think of some more of his favourites while Esme charged around the caravan piling up a bowl for him.

'And do you like ice cream, Inspector?' Cosmo asked. 'You look like a man with very good taste.'

'Yes, I like it a great deal. In fact, I would say that I was something of an ice-cream expert.' The inspector patted his stomach smugly.

Esme placed the overflowing sweets in front of the inspector and dragged Cosmo into the caravan.

'I've got an idea. You
can see the Pirate Circus
from here. If we can keep
him here long enough he'll
see that they have animals
there. Then he'll have to believe us and close
them down instead of us.' Esme put her head
in her hands. There was only so much that
they could feed him, and the Pirate Circus
show didn't start for another hour.

'I know, let's have an ice-cream sundae
contest and he can be the judge,' said Cosmo.
Although obviously it's just for show because
I'm bound to win! I will prove that my Choco
Toffee Honey Ginger Crunch Supremo is ice-
cream sundae of the year, and far better than
yours.'

'Good idea, but we'd better ask him first!'

'OK, OK!' Cosmo jumped the steps.

'Excuse me, Inspector, we were just wondering whether, as an expert on the subject, you would be willing to judge an ice-cream contest? Would you help us?'

With the inspector sitting comfortably outside, Esme and Cosmo switched on the ice-cream machine. Esme pulled down her notebook with all her own recipes written in and found the page for Space Hopper Sherbet Sundae Extraordinaire.

Cosmo threw out the ingredients he could remember from the last time he had made up the Choco Toffee Honey Ginger Crunch Supremo and started to pour cream into the ice-cream machine.

strawberry liquorice stick

popping space dust

flying saucer sherbet sprinkles

Whipped cream

Sparkling orange cream sorbet

fizzy cherry cola bottles

space popping meringues

Whipped cream

Lemon Sherbet Sorbet

Tiny fizzy Toffee apples

'Who said that you could go first?' Esme asked.

'Do you want my help or not?' Cosmo replied.

'Don't throw eggs at Cosmo's head, don't throw eggs at Cosmo's head. Think of the circus, think of the circus,' she repeated quietly to herself as she started to whisk the exploding space dust into the egg whites ready for the meringues.

FOURTEEN
★ ★ ★

Pirates and
Ice Cream

Word travelled around the circus that the inspector had arrived and as he stuck the extra-long spoon that he had been given into the Choco Toffee Honey Ginger Crunch Supremo, the whole of Circus Miranda came out to see if there was anything they could do to help.

Music from the Pirate Circus started up and crowds gathered outside the ship.

Everyone hoped that the inspector was a slow eater.

'Delicious,' called the inspector after crunching through layers of home-made caramel and freshly baked ginger biscuits crumbled over chocolate ice cream with toffee pieces. He smacked his lips as he dug down to a warm pool of vanilla honey nestled at the very bottom of the glass.

'I'm ready for the next one,' the inspector said, looking towards Esme expectantly.

Esme pulled the freshly baked meringues out of the oven and poured sherbet, cream, eggs and sugar into the ice-cream machine.

'It won't be long, Inspector,' Esme called. 'Perhaps you'd like a slice of cherry bakewell pie while you're waiting?'

'Yes, cherry bakewell and a cup of tea between courses would be fine. It will clear

my palate, I'm sure.' The inspector looked up at the all the circus acts gazing hopefully towards the river.

'What's over there?' he asked.

'The Pirate Circus,' said Magnus. 'It's about to start. Down on the river. Shall we move your table over this way a little so that you can watch it while you wait?'

'Yes, please,' said the inspector. 'A little light entertainment will go very well with my tea and cake.'

Esme delivered the cake to the inspector and poured out his tea just as the pirate acrobats clambered up the masts of the ship and began their routine.

'There, just as I said – no animals.' The inspector took a large bite of the tart.

Out came the tumbling pirates, somersaulting off the side of the boat. Circus Miranda watched and waited as the inspector finished off the rest of the tart in two large bites.

'I'm ready for the next sundae now. If it isn't here very soon I shall have to close this place down and go. I have a very important job to do. I can't just sit around waiting all day.' The inspector wiped his chin impatiently.

Esme added the last peak of sherbet cream to the towering Space Hopper Sherbet Sundae Extraordinaire and came out to place it in front of the inspector.

His spoon slid through the sherbet cream, crackled through the space-dust

meringues and slipped into the sparkling lemon sorbet. He had just burrowed down for a fizzy toffee apple when the Pirate Circus animals were finally dragged out to perform.

'Goodness, I must say this is really most extraordinary,' said the inspector.

Esme's spirits soared. The plan was working. Now he would see the badly treated animals and have to admit he was wrong and close down the other circus instead.

'Absolutely extraordinary.' The inspector stuck his head deeper into the glass, desperately rooting around for another of the delicious, tastebud-tickling fizzy toffee apples.

'Get his head out of there,' howled Esme. 'He's going to miss it!'

In response to Esme's cry for help, the

other Circus Miranda performers started to
clap loudly and cheer as though something
very exciting was going on and finally the
nosy inspector pulled his head out of the
glass and looked up.

He leapt to his feet.

'Are those animals?' he cried.

'At the Pirate Circus!' he shouted. 'How dare they . . . they tricked me. I will not be made a fool of. I am going down there right now to close them down.' He turned towards the pirate ship.

'But who won the ice-cream contest?' Cosmo asked, standing in his way.

'COSMO!' Esme yelled. 'Let him go!'

'But I want to know who won.' Cosmo stood firm. 'It was me, wasn't it, Inspector?'

The inspector picked up his clipboard and wrote down a name. He folded up the piece of paper and handed it to Cosmo before marching past him.

FIFTEEN
★ ★ ★

Parties and Partings

At that evening's celebration, Esme sat and fed Donk marshmallows that had been

toasted on Mallow's horn. 'I'm so happy that you're OK again, Donk. And you too, Mallow.'

The circus formed a parade behind Esme and Donk as they went to wave the boys off in the hot air balloon. Her parents walked with them, each with an arm around Esme's shoulders.

On the way there Esme remembered the ice-cream contest. She'd been so delighted they'd saved the circus that she'd forgotten all about it.

Her parents had returned just in time to see the inspector leave and the whole of Circus

Miranda had watched as the Pirate Circus had been closed down and the animals brought up for the boys to take back to Maclinkey Castle to be cared for properly.

'Cosmo, whose name did he write on the paper?' Esme asked.

'Mine, of course,' said Cosmo. 'Obviously.'

'I don't believe you,' said Esme. 'Where's the paper?'

'Oh, I don't know. I've lost it,' Cosmo replied. 'Bad luck, Esme. Next time I see you, you have to do all my jobs for two days.' Cosmo flicked Donk's ear and clambered into the balloon basket.

The white Siberian tiger climbed in next and then the other animals, and finally Magnus helped Gus in with their suitcases.

'All ready,' called Magnus, firing up the
gas as they released the ropes.

'See you next summer!' called Esme.

'Eeeaawwww eeeaaawww,' hooted Donk.

The balloon stayed where it was.

'Why aren't they going?' asked Esme.

'COSMO!' shouted Magnus as he looked more closely at Cosmo's bulging pockets. 'Throw those sweets overboard. You're too heavy and we can't take off!'

'No,' said Cosmo. 'I made them and they are coming home with me. Don't make me leave them.'

'Throw them overboard or I will throw you overboard,' replied Magnus.

'Can't we leave some of the animals instead? They weigh more than the sweets. If we weren't taking the tiger back we could take all the sweets in the caravan.'

'Cosmo, Dad told us to bring the white Siberian tiger back to Maclinkey Castle with us! I will leave you before I leave him,'

Magnus said, losing patience.

'Fine then,' said Cosmo, throwing one small fruit drop over the side.

Magnus glared at him.

'Gus loves it here. Let's leave Gus.'

Cosmo went to help Gus out over the side of the basket.

'We are not leaving Gus! Cosmo, this is your last chance.' Magnus fired up the gas to try again.

The basket stayed still.

Cosmo took out a chocolate éclair, then one more and another until the balloon finally began to lift into the air.

'Keep going or you're going over,' shouted Magnus.

Cosmo carried on emptying out his

pockets – lemon bonbons, cola bottles, sherbet fizzes, flying saucers, creamy caramels and strawberry chews rained down on the village below and in the middle of the sweet shower floated down a scruffy piece of paper with the name Esme written on it.

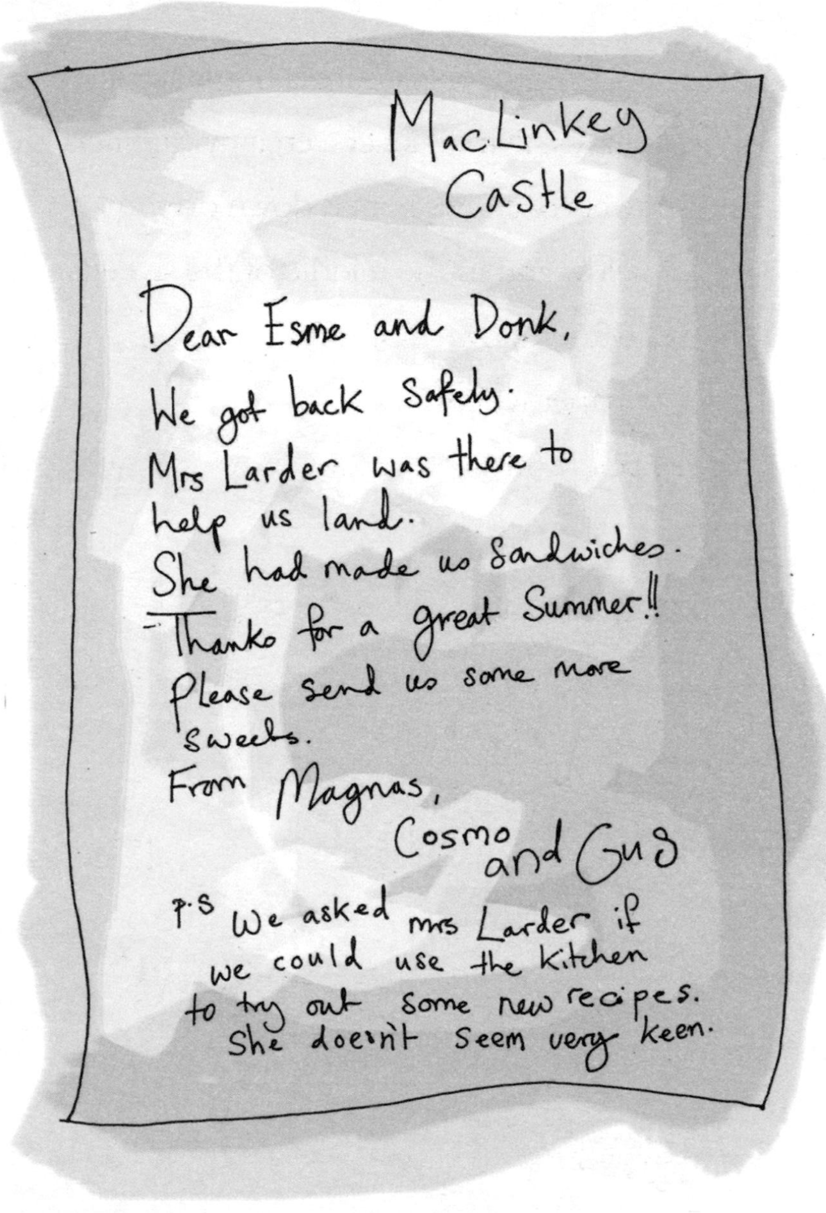

MacLinkey
Castle

Dear Esme and Donk,

We got back safely.
Mrs Larder was there to
help us land.
She had made us sandwiches.
Thanks for a great summer!!
Please send us some more
sweets.
From Magnus,
        Cosmo
           and Gus

P.S We asked mrs Larder if
we could use the kitchen
to try out some new recipes.
She doesn't seem very keen.

My
Summer
at the
Circus
by
Gus.

Donk
Showed
Me
how

My
Clown
Make-up

My
favourite
Circus acts

The amazing Horse Jugglers

donk

flying tigers

Esme

Welcome to

Make our own circus

Esme + Donk

ESME'S Activity BOOK

if you like my activity book the sheets are available to download online at www.amazingesme.com

not good drawing

my best ideas

Your own circus

Write programme ?

Can you make up a programme for your fantasy circus? What would the acts be?

Can you write some information about each of the acts and draw them?

PHOTOGRAPH © ANNA NOWINSKA-BOARDMAN

TAMARA MACFARLANE

As a child Tamara practically lived in bookshops. She continued her love-affair with reading whilst studying English and Education, specialising in Children's Literature at university.

After a number of years spent as a literacy co-ordinator, Tamara had her first child and decided she would like to live in a children's bookshop again.

As she couldn't find one that she liked, she founded the award-winning *Tales on Moon Lane* bookshop in Herne Hill, filling it with all her favourite books.

One day, she noticed a gap in the shelves in the 5-8 year-old section and, being unable to find many books that she loved, she started to write them herself. That is when *Amazing Esme* turned up!

Introducing
BOOK
1

AMAZING ESME

WELCOME
to Esme Miranda's Fairground Circus

GASP AT THE WONDROUS
UNICORNED PIG

Come, see the amazing
DIVING WEASLES

Marvel at the
PIROUETTING DONKEY

Laugh yourself silly at a
BAD MANNERED TEA PARTY

Witness a
FOOD-FLINGING EXTRAVAGANZA